But That is Not Me!

SUSAN LARSON KIDD
PHOTOS BY **RICHARD HOEG**

One day, Harry the Hairy woodpecker asked his sky friends...

What Should I do?

You should flit to the feeder and back to the maple tree.

That's what I do, said the Chickadee.

But that is not me, said Harry.

You should hop on the ground and catch worms.

That's what I do, said the Robin.

But that is not me, said Harry.

You Should Sit on the ground where all the extra Seeds fall.

That's what I do,
Said the Junco.

But that is not me,
Said Harry.

You should walk on the tree upside down.

That's what I do,
said the Nuthatch.

But that is not me,
said Harry.

You should sit on the top of the trees and sing loudly.

That's what I do,
said the Mockingbird.

But that is not me,
said Harry.

You should pause at the flower and sip nectar.

That's what I do,
said the Hummingbird.

But that is not me,
said Harry.

You Should coo with your partner at the edge of the woods.

That's what I do,
Said the Mourning Dove.

But that is not me,
Said Harry.

You should float down to the water to catch a fish.

That's what I do, said the Osprey.

But that is not me, said Harry.

You should land on the fence rail and strike a pose.

That's what I do, said the Blue Jay.

But that is not me, said Harry.

You should soar through the open sky in flight.

That's what I do,
said the Bald Eagle.

But that is not me,
said Harry.

You should call to your mate with a sweet sounding song.

That's what I do,
said the Cardinal.

But that is not me,
said Harry.

You Should carry cattail fluff to make your nest.

That's what I do,
Said the Red-winged Blackbird.

But that is Not Me,
Said Harry.

You should stand very still at the edge of the lake.

That's what I do,
Said the Great Blue Heron.

But that is not me,
Said Harry.

THEN WHAT SHOULD YOU DO?!

They all asked Harry.

I should drum out my rhythm on the trunk of a tree and be ever so happy just to be me!

For Bailey and *Max*—
May your animal totems guide your way safely through life's journey
—Susan Larson Kidd

For All my Grandchildren—
No matter your age, may you always hear the joy of bird song
—Richard Hoeg

A NOTE FROM THE AUTHOR...
I wrote this picture book for young children and children with disabilities. It is repetitive and predictable to encourage choral response of early readers. It includes real photographs not only to teach of birds' natural beauty and need for preservation, but also to be more concrete for those with cognitive differences.

All the beautiful birds in this story may be seen in the Northeastern region of Minnesota. In honoring of Native American tradition, birds are animal totems. Often, when the Hairy Woodpecker shows up to someone, he carries a message of the importance of being yourself (Andrews, 2002). That is the simple theme of this story.

Andrews, T. (2002). *Animal Speak*. Woodbury, MN: Llewellyn Publications.

Visit us online to learn more about birding with children... www.365DaysOfBirds.com/birding-with-children/

Thanks to Sparky Stensaas of Stone Ridge Press for adding his design touch to this book.

Happy Endings Publishing
Dr SLK Consulting, LLC

BUT THAT IS NOT ME!

ISBN-13: 978-0-692-87428-8 (softcover)